THIS BOOK BELONGS TO

....

LITTLE RED RIDING HOOD

Written by Helen Anderton

Illustrated by Stuart Lynch

make believe ideas

Reading together

This book is designed to be fun for children who are gaining confidence in their reading. They will enjoy and benefit from some time discussing the story with an adult. Here are some ways you can help your child take those first steps in reading:

* Encourage your child to look at the pictures and talk about what is happening in the story.

* Help your child to find familiar words and sound out the letters in harder words.

* Ask your child to read and repeat each short sentence.

Look at rhymes

Many of the sentences in this book are simple rhymes. Encourage your child to recognise rhyming words. Try asking the following questions:

* What does this word say?

* Can you find a word that rhymes with it?

* Look at the ending of two words that rhyme. Are they spelt the same? For example, "black" and "back", and "could" and "hood".

Reading activities

The **What happens next?** activity encourages your child to retell the story and point to the mixed-up pictures in the right order.

The **Rhyming words** activity takes six words from the story and asks your child to read and find other words that rhyme with them.

The **Key words** pages provide practice with common words used in the context of the book. Read the sentences with your child and encourage him or her to make up more sentences using the key words listed around the border.

A **Picture dictionary** page asks children to focus closely on nine words from the story. Encourage your child to look carefully at each word, cover it with his or her hand, write it on a separate piece of paper, and finally, check it!

Do not complete all the activities at once – doing one each time you read will ensure that your child continues to enjoy the story and the time you are spending together. Have fun!

There once was a smart but shy little girl
who wore a red cape to hide her curls.
She thought they were horrid! No one understood –
they just called her Little Red Riding Hood.

Little Red's granny had got very sick.

She needed some pills and a walking stick.

She lived in a cottage, deep in the wood,

and she loved her Little Red Riding Hood.

Said Red to her mum, "Please let me see Gran."

"Of course," Mum said. "What an excellent plan!"

Mum packed for Gran all the food she could,

to be sent with Little Red Riding Hood.

Little Red's mum said, "Beware how you go.
    Don't speak to strangers and don't dawdle so!"
Then over the gate and into the wood
    skipped innocent Little Red Riding Hood.

But a nasty wolf had spied Little Red.

"Where are you going so quickly?" he said.

"To dear Granny's cottage, here in the wood,"
squeaked terrified Little Red Riding Hood.

13

Wolf dashed away with an idea in mind.

At Granny's cottage he knew what he'd find!

If his brilliant plan worked as it should,

soon he could EAT Little Red Riding Hood.

On tiptoes Wolf crept to Granny's front door
and went straight in (hearing Granny's loud snore).

He swallowed her whole – because he could!
Then waited for Little Red Riding Hood.

Red rang the bell when she reached Granny's home.

"Come in, dear," she heard (in Wolf's growly tone).

"Why, Granny, your eyes look bigger!" Red cried.

"The better to SEE you with," Wolf replied.

"And, Granny, your ears look bigger – and black!"
   "The better to HEAR you with," Wolf said back.
"And, Granny, your teeth look much bigger, too!"
   Roared Wolf, "All the better for ME to eat YOU!"

Wolf gobbled Red and his belly grew round!
Meanwhile a woodsman had tracked the wolf down . . .

He sliced the wolf open – there Granny stood,
and with her was Little Red Riding Hood!

23

From then on, the girl wasn't shy anymore
about showing the curls she had hated before.
She taught wolves manners and how to be good,
and threw out that silly red riding hood!

IT'S NICE TO BE nice!

What happens next?

Some of the pictures from the story have been mixed up! Can you retell the story and point to each picture in the correct order?

Rhyming words

Read the words in the middle of each group and point to the other words that rhyme with them.

bed

bread

red

cape

ear

plan

quick

stick

shy

thick

gate

good

hood

stood

wolf

bell

gran

little

man

plan

feet

eat

good

sweet

teeth

curls

belly

granny

jelly

smelly

Now choose a word and make up a rhyming chant!

There is **smelly jelly** in my **belly**!

Key words

These sentences use common words to describe the story. Read the sentences and then make up new sentences for the other words in the border.

Little Red didn't **like** her curly hair.

Granny got **very** sick.

Little Red went to **see** her Granny.

Wolf **had** a plan.

Wolf pretended to **be** Granny.

like · very · not

· are · but · help · with · all · we · can · his · up · had ·

When Wolf ate Little Red, his belly grew round.

A woodsman came to **help**.

The woodsman saved Little Red and **her** Granny.

Little Red was **not** shy anymore.

Little Red taught wolves **to** be good.

the · and · a · to · see · in · he · I · of · it · too · you · they · on · she · is · for · at

my · her · when · there · out · this · have · so · be ·

Picture dictionary

Look carefully at the pictures and the words.
Now cover the words, one at a time.
Can you remember how to write them?

cottage

curls

food

granny

hood

teeth

wolf

wood

woodsman